COLIN THOMPSON
PICTURES OF HOME

GREEN TIGER PRESS

Published by Simon & Schuster

New York · London · Toronto · Sydney · Tokyo · Singapore

For Heather

GREEN TIGER PRESS
Simon & Schuster Building, Rockefeller Center
1230 Avenue of the Americas, New York, New York 10020
Copyright © 1992 by Colin Thompson
All rights reserved including the right of reproduction
in whole or in part in any form.
Originally published in Great Britain by Julia MacRae Books,
a division of the Random Century Group Ltd.
First U.S. edition 1993
GREEN TIGER PRESS is an imprint of Simon & Schuster.
Manufactured in Singapore.

10 9 8 7 6 5 4 3 2 1

Library of Congress Cataloging-in-Publication Data
Thompson, Colin (Colin Edward)   Pictures of home / Colin Thompson.
p.   cm.   Summary: An illustrated collection of quotations
by children about the meaning of home.   1. Home—Quotations,
maxims, etc.—Juvenile literature.   2. Children—Quotations.
[1. Home.   2. Children's writings.]   I. Title.   PN6084.H57T47
1993   811′.540809282—dc20   92-11359   CIP
ISBN: 0-671-79584-8

The pictures in this book were originally commissioned by
Leeds Permanent Building Society
for their calendars of 1990, 1991 and 1992
and are reproduced here with their kind permission.

Thanks to the children of Upperby Junior School, Carlisle, England,
for the writing and haiku verses in this book.

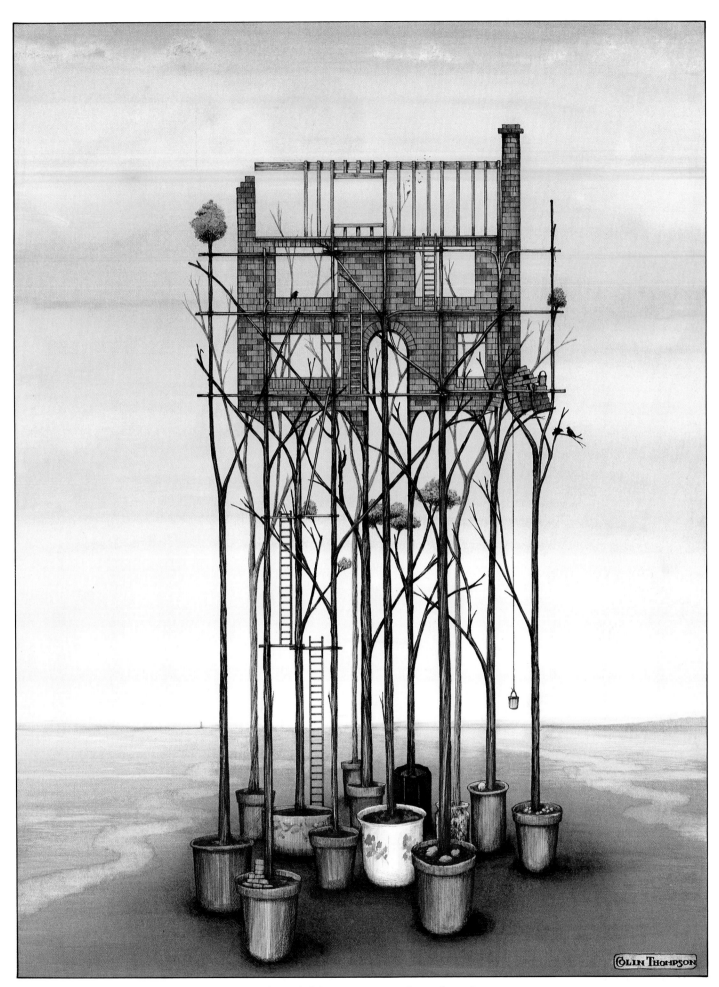

Every home should have a roof and a door. *Zoe, 11*

Some houses are big.
Other houses are quite small.
Others are just right.
David, 11

Home means somewhere to turn to. *Sarah Jane, 11*

Houses are buildings
where people enjoy their life
and they are comfy.
Andrew, 11

A home is love and
care because your parents love
you and care for you.
Douglas, 10

A garden is where nature lives. *Lindsay, 11*

Home is mom and dad.
Home is TV and the fridge.
Home is going to bed.
Stuart, 10

I love home. It is
lovely and warm. I like home,
it is where you grow.
Kimberly, 10

Every home should have a heart. *Daniel, 10*

A house is a place where someone else lives.
A home is my home.
Lisa, 11

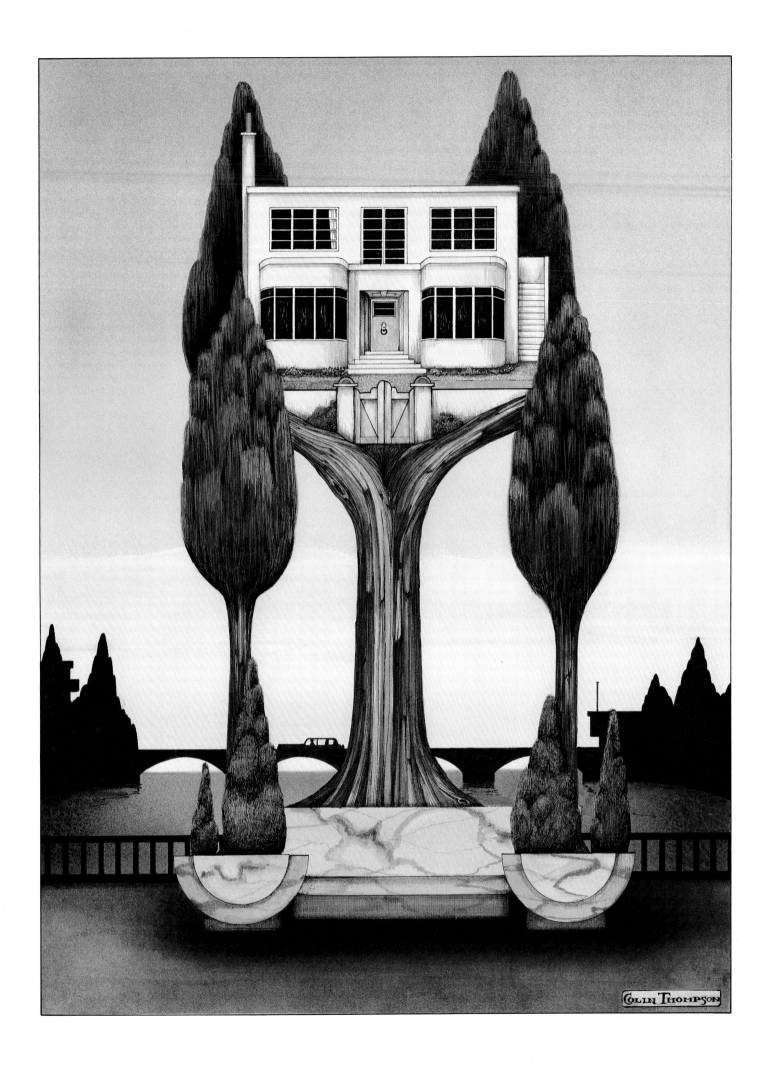

What I really like about home
is that it will always be there and never go away.
Leanne, 10

A garden is a place where your house is in the middle of. *Stacey, 11*

Home is a place where people love you.
Natalie, 11

Home is a nice place.
Home should have two computers.
My dad is quite cool.
Tony, 11

What I really love about home
is you don't have to pay for your dinner.
David, 11

Every home should have a friend and someone to care for. *Douglas, 10*

Home is my parents.
You should have love in all homes.
Love is my parents.
Ian, 10

Home is the best place.
When I think of home I think
of my best kittens.
Richard, 10

Houses are cozy.
They are dry when you are wet.
Small houses are best.
Michael, 11

Home means where you grow up. *Kimberly, 10*

Houses are made out
of bricks and if they were made
of sand they would fall.
Kerry, 10

Home is where I live.
Home is where I'm loved and cared
for, by my mom most.

Carley, 10

I walk down the road
and I see all the houses.
Some are big, some small.
Jodie, 11

My dream home would be where I live now. *Tony, 11*

Houses are where you
live and where your mom and dad
are waiting for you.
Douglas, 10